LOOK FOR LISA: TIME TRAVELER

By
Anthony Tallarico

SMITHMARK

Copyright © 1992 Kidsbooks Inc. and Anthony Tallarico
7004 N. California Ave.
Chicago, IL 60645

ISBN: 0-8317-9317-1

This edition published in 1992 by SMITHMARK Publishers Inc.,
112 Madison Avenue, New York, NY 10016

SMITHMARK books are available for bulk purchase for sales promotion and premium use.
For details write or telephone the Manager of Special Sales, SMITHMARK Publishers Inc.,
112 Madison Avenue, New York, NY 10016. (212) 532-6600.
Manufactured in the United States of America

Lisa is going on an exciting adventure in her time-travel submarine and she wants you to come along!

LOOK FOR LISA IN PREHISTORIC TIMES AND…

- ☑ Balloons (2)
- ☑ Bathtub
- ☑ Book
- ☑ Boot
- ☑ Bottle
- ☑ Broom
- ☐ Candle
- ☐ Clown
- ☐ Coffee pot
- ☑ Cup
- ☑ Egg
- ☐ Football
- ☐ Four-leaf clover
- ☐ Hammer
- ☐ Hockey stick
- ☐ Ice-cream cone
- ☐ Ladder
- ☐ Lamp
- ☐ Necktie
- ☐ Pizza
- ☐ Ring
- ☐ Scarecrow
- ☐ Sock
- ☐ Stars (2)
- ☐ String of pearls
- ☐ Sunglasses
- ☐ Tent
- ☐ Toothbrush
- ☐ Top hat
- ☐ Umbrella
- ☐ Used tire
- ☐ Wristwatch

What hasn't been invented yet?
What's in the cup?
Is there anything for rent?

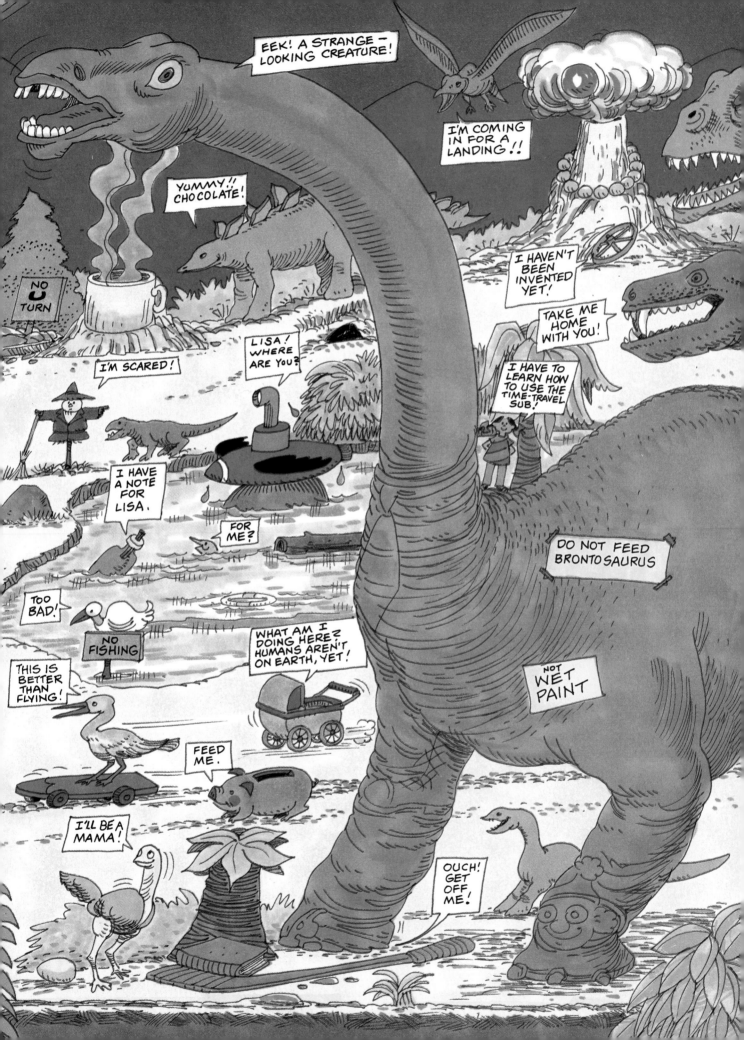

Lisa has gone forward in time and she's landed in Count Dracula's home in Transylvania.

LOOK FOR LISA IN THIS CREEPY CASTLE AND...

- ☐ Axe
- ☐ Baseball
- ☐ Bones (6)
- ☐ Books (2)
- ☐ Boomerang
- ☐ Candles (6)
- ☐ Cracked mirror
- ☐ Dart
- ☐ Dustpan
- ☐ Envelope
- ☐ Fish
- ☐ Fish skeleton
- ☐ Heart
- ☐ Keys (3)
- ☐ Mallet
- ☐ Mice (4)
- ☐ Needle
- ☐ Number 13
- ☐ Pickles
- ☐ Rabbit
- ☐ Ring
- ☐ Roller skate
- ☐ Screwdriver
- ☐ Shovel
- ☐ Skateboard
- ☐ Skulls (5)
- ☐ Spoon
- ☐ Stake
- ☐ Steak
- ☐ Sword
- ☐ Tick-tack-toe
- ☐ Top hat
- ☐ Wind-up car
- ☐ Witch's hat
- ☐ Worms (2)
- ☐ Zipper

What is Uncle Nutzy?
What year is it?
Where is the garlic?

Next, Lisa travels to the year 1752. She's watching Benjamin Franklin as he proves that lightning is a form of electricity.

LOOK FOR LISA AT THIS HISTORIC HAPPENING AND...

☐ Arrow
☐ Basket
☐ Bell
☐ Bifocal eyeglasses
☐ Brushes (2)
☐ Bucket
☐ Cane
☐ Corn
☐ Deer
☐ Drums (2)
☐ Fish
☐ Flowerpot
☐ Frog
☐ Ghost
☐ Grapes
☐ Hair bows (5)
☐ Hammer
☐ Hearts (2)
☐ Hoop
☐ Keys (2)
☐ Kites (2)
☐ Ladder
☐ Mushroom
☐ Pumpkin
☐ Rabbit
☐ Ring
☐ Snail
☐ Snake
☐ Stamp
☐ Stars (3)
☐ Surfboard
☐ Tepee
☐ Turtle
☐ Umbrellas (3)
☐ Worm

What is Mrs. Franklin's first name?
What is the name of Franklin's almanac?

Wow! The time-travel sub has landed in the middle of the Ed Sullivan show where the Beatles are performing in America for the first time.

LOOK FOR LISA AS SHE ROCKS AND ROLLS AND...

- ☐ Balloons (2)
- ☐ Banjo
- ☐ Baton
- ☐ Bird
- ☐ Book
- ☐ Bow tie
- ☐ Bubblegum bubble
- ☐ Candle
- ☐ Chef
- ☐ Count Dracula
- ☐ Cymbals
- ☐ Dog
- ☐ Earmuffs
- ☐ Envelope
- ☐ Eyeglasses (3)
- ☐ Flower
- ☐ Football
- ☐ Ghost
- ☐ Giraffe
- ☐ Hearts (2)
- ☐ Kite
- ☐ Mouse
- ☐ Party hat
- ☐ Police officer
- ☐ Propeller
- ☐ Pumpkin
- ☐ Rabbit
- ☐ Skateboard
- ☐ Snowman
- ☐ Star
- ☐ Straw hat
- ☐ Tin man
- ☐ Wagon
- ☐ Witch
- ☐ Yo-yo

How many TV cameras are there? Where were the Beatles from?

Lisa travels to Paris, France next, and arrives in the year 1902. She's in the laboratory of the first great female scientist, Madame Marie Curie.

LOOK FOR LISA AMONG THESE EXCITING EXPERIMENTS AND...

☐ Birds (2)
☐ Bone
☐ Book
☐ Broom
☐ Butterfly
☐ Cactus
☐ Candle
☐ Candy cane
☐ Carrot
☐ Clothespin
☐ Comb
☐ Compass
☐ Feather
☐ Ghost
☐ Hearts (2)
☐ Hot dog
☐ Ice-cream cone
☐ Igloo
☐ Keys (2)
☐ Mouse
☐ Nail
☐ Painted egg
☐ Pear
☐ Pencil
☐ Pie
☐ Rocket ship
☐ Roller skate
☐ Scissors
☐ Slice of pizza
☐ Straw
☐ Thermometer
☐ Toothbrush
☐ Tweezers

What is not dry yet?
What kind of pie is it?

Astronaut Neil Armstrong takes "a giant leap for mankind," as he thinks he's the first person to set foot on the moon. Little does he know, Lisa beat him to the moon walk!

LOOK FOR LISA IN THESE CAVERNOUS CRATERS AND...

- ☐ Airplane
- ☐ Apple
- ☐ Bat
- ☐ Book
- ☐ Bottle
- ☐ Camel
- ☐ Can
- ☐ Cat
- ☐ Chicken
- ☐ Cow
- ☐ Crown
- ☐ Dog
- ☐ Drum
- ☐ Flower
- ☐ Football
- ☐ Ghost
- ☐ Guitar
- ☐ Hammer
- ☐ Ice-cream cone
- ☐ Lips
- ☐ Mitten
- ☐ Owl
- ☐ Paintbrush
- ☐ Penguin
- ☐ Purse
- ☐ Rabbit
- ☐ Sailboat
- ☐ Seal
- ☐ Snake
- ☐ Stars (4)
- ☐ Tent
- ☐ Top hat
- ☐ Tree
- ☐ Umbrella
- ☐ Wreath

Can you find at least 12 more hidden things?

Lisa decides she wants her next trip to be a quiet sea voyage. But her time machine must have had something else in mind because Lisa has landed right in the middle of Captain Ahab's pursuit of Moby Dick!

LOOK FOR LISA IN THE OCEAN AND...

- ☐ Balloons (2)
- ☐ Beach ball
- ☐ Book
- ☐ Boomerang
- ☐ Bottle
- ☐ Candle
- ☐ Chef's hat
- ☐ Clown
- ☐ Drum
- ☐ Fire hydrant
- ☐ Fork
- ☐ Harp
- ☐ Harpoon
- ☐ Kerosene lamp
- ☐ Kite
- ☐ Lost sock
- ☐ Lunch box
- ☐ Mallet
- ☐ Mermaid
- ☐ Merman
- ☐ Oars (5)
- ☐ Pencil
- ☐ Picture frame
- ☐ Quarter moon
- ☐ Saw
- ☐ Shark fins (2)
- ☐ Spoon
- ☐ Stingray
- ☐ Stork
- ☐ Surfboard
- ☐ Telephone
- ☐ Tree
- ☐ Turtle
- ☐ Umbrella

What is the name of the whaling ship?

Lisa's time machine has traveled to a wedding party in the 1760s. Who's getting married? It's someone you may have heard of.

LOOK FOR LISA AT THIS SPECIAL CELEBRATION AND...

- ☐ Apple
- ☐ Arrow
- ☐ Banana
- ☐ Basket
- ☐ Boom box
- ☐ Broken wheel
- ☐ Broom
- ☐ Brush
- ☐ Elf
- ☐ Fiddle
- ☐ Fishing pole
- ☐ Flowerpot
- ☐ Fork
- ☐ Frog
- ☐ Gift
- ☐ Ice-cream cone
- ☐ Key
- ☐ Loaf of bread
- ☐ Mushroom
- ☐ Pear
- ☐ Pizza delivery
- ☐ Portable telephone
- ☐ Pumpkins (3)
- ☐ Rabbit
- ☐ Scarecrow
- ☐ Sherlock Holmes
- ☐ Skateboard
- ☐ Snake
- ☐ Soup
- ☐ Squirrel
- ☐ Top hat
- ☐ Wagons (2)
- ☐ Wedding cake
- ☐ Wooden spoon

What is Mrs. Boone's first name? What's wrong with the table?

Lisa is now visiting the famous inventor, Thomas Edison, in his laboratory. Do you know some of the wonderful things he invented?

LOOK FOR LISA IN THE "WIZARD OF MENLO PARK'S" LAB AND...

- ☐ Ball
- ☐ Baseball cap
- ☐ Bird
- ☐ Bone
- ☐ Book
- ☐ Bucket
- ☐ Candle
- ☐ Doughnut
- ☐ Duck
- ☐ Feather
- ☐ Hard hat
- ☐ Hot dog
- ☐ Kerosene lamp
- ☐ Light bulb
- ☐ Milk container
- ☐ Mouse
- ☐ Pencils (2)
- ☐ Phonograph
- ☐ Picture frame
- ☐ Pillow
- ☐ Poodle
- ☐ Pumpkin
- ☐ Roller skates
- ☐ Safe
- ☐ Sailor's hat
- ☐ Screwdriver
- ☐ Ship
- ☐ Star
- ☐ Stool
- ☐ Sunglasses
- ☐ Typewriter
- ☐ Umbrella
- ☐ Wastepaper basket
- ☐ Wheel

What is the name of Edison's film? Who can't read?

Lisa has pushed a few too many buttons and *zap-ping-kabaa* she's landed on a distant planet in the future!

LOOK FOR LISA AMONGST THESE FRIENDLY ALIENS AND...

- ☐ Apple
- ☐ Arrow
- ☐ Balloon
- ☐ Banana
- ☐ Bicycle horn
- ☐ Biplane
- ☐ Bone
- ☐ Bowling ball
- ☐ Bucket
- ☐ Captain Hook
- ☐ Clothespin
- ☐ Comb
- ☐ Cup
- ☐ Door
- ☐ Feather
- ☐ Fire hydrants (2)
- ☐ Flying saucer
- ☐ Football
- ☐ Guitar
- ☐ Heart
- ☐ Hot dog
- ☐ Ice skate
- ☐ Lock
- ☐ Nut
- ☐ Party hat
- ☐ Pie
- ☐ Sled
- ☐ Slice of pizza
- ☐ Slice of watermelon
- ☐ Space traffic cop
- ☐ Spoon
- ☐ Tepee
- ☐ Tire
- ☐ Watering can

What game is "it" late for?
What needs a target?

Lisa is trying to get back to our time zone. She's close…it's now 1925 and she's on stage at the Hippodrome Theater in New York City with the famous magician, Houdini.

LOOK FOR LISA BEFORE SHE DISAPPEARS AND…

- ☐ Balloon
- ☐ Baseball cap
- ☐ Bat
- ☐ Big apple
- ☐ Birds (2)
- ☐ Cane
- ☐ Carrot
- ☐ Chef
- ☐ Clown
- ☐ Count Dracula
- ☐ Crown
- ☐ Drum
- ☐ Duck
- ☐ Fish (2)
- ☐ Flowerpot
- ☐ Giraffe
- ☐ Graduate
- ☐ Helmet
- ☐ Jack-in-the-box
- ☐ Key
- ☐ Lion
- ☐ Mirror
- ☐ Palm tree
- ☐ Pig
- ☐ Ring
- ☐ Sailboat
- ☐ Sailor's hat
- ☐ Sled
- ☐ Snake
- ☐ Stars (5)
- ☐ Toothbrush
- ☐ Truck
- ☐ Whale

What did Houdini do in Australia? Where is the rabbit going?

Lisa has finally made it! She's back home with all of her "Where Are They?" friends.

LOOK FOR LISA AND...

- ☐ Bats (2)
- ☐ Bones (2)
- ☐ Clouds (3)
- ☐ Gift
- ☐ Hammers (2)
- ☐ Hearts (3)
- ☐ Hose
- ☐ Oar
- ☐ Octopus
- ☐ Question mark
- ☐ Stars (5)
- ☐ Sunglasses (3)
- ☐ Tulip
- ☐ Turtle
- ☐ Watering can

Who knew where Lisa was?

LOOK FOR LISA